ADAM'S ATOMIC ADVENTURES

Adam's Atomic Adventures

Alice L. Baxter

iUniverse, Inc.

New York Lincoln Shanghai

Adam's Atomic Adventures

Copyright © 2007 by Alice L. Baxter

iUniverse books may be ordered through booksellers or by contacting:

iUniverse
2021 Pine Lake Road, Suite 100
Lincoln, NE 68512
www.iuniverse.com
1-800-Authors (1-800-288-4677)

Because of the dynamic nature of the Internet, any Web addresses or links contained in this book may have changed since publication and may no longer be valid.

This is a work of fiction. All of the characters, names, incidents, organizations, and dialogue in this novel are either the products of the author's imagination or are used fictitiously.

Cover illustration by Christine MacClintic

ISBN: 978-0-595-45616-1 (pbk)
ISBN: 978-0-595-89917-3 (ebk)

Printed in the United States of America

To Gwen, Sarah, Dick and Tim
For honest advice and endless support

Chapter One

"Come on, Adam, it wasn't your fault." Sam plopped down next to his friend, who sat slumped on the bench, his head hanging between his knees. "You did a great job, and there was no way anyone on our team was going to get a shot past their new goalie."

Adam did not answer, staring intently at the lone patch of stubby grass poking through the dirt under the home team bench. Sam looked anxiously at the schoolyard. A handful of stragglers were making their way to the main door. He checked his watch.

"We've got to get back to class," Sam said.

Without responding to Sam, Adam slowly lifted one foot and began picking grass out of his cleats. Sam stood and paced in front of the bench. Finally, Adam looked up, his shaggy blond hair half-covering his blue eyes.

"How can I face the team? I've been warming the bench for weeks now, praying for a chance to play, and what happens? The coach finally sends me in, and I blow it. I had a clear shot, Sam, and there is just no excuse for missing."

"Don't feel so bad, Adam. There's another game tomorrow," Sam said. "You'll have another chance."

"What are you talking about, Sam?" Adam almost shouted. "Look at me. I'm the shortest boy in the fifth grade, and there's no way the coach is going to give me another chance. He only put me in today because Danny was out sick. Do you really think he will risk it again tomorrow? Not a chance. This piece of bench has my name on it for the rest of the season." Adam stood up and kicked the bench, almost knocking it over.

"But you're the fastest runner on the team, Adam."

"As if anyone cares," Adam snapped. "What good does it do if everyone thinks I'm too small to compete?"

Sam didn't know what to say. He and Adam had been best friends since first grade, when they were about the same height and wore the same size shoes. They still could share sneakers, but Adam's feet looked way too big for his thin legs, while Sam's feet were perfectly proportioned for a sturdy body that towered six inches over Adam. Sam could only imagine how awful it was to ride the bench. He had started every soccer game since the team was formed. He wanted to reassure Adam, but in his heart, he knew Adam was right. Tomorrow his friend would be right back at the end of the bench. Sam scanned the empty playground.

"Adam, the bell is going to ring any second now. You don't want to get in trouble for being late again."

"I don't care," Adam grumbled. "No one will miss me."

Sam looked at his watch again. "You know that's not true. And remember how much Mrs. Gold hates it when kids are late?"

Just then the bell rang.

"C'mon Adam. I know you feel awful, but why make things worse by getting yelled at by Mrs. Gold? Let's not risk having to stay after school." Sam started to walk away from the soccer field, looking over his shoulder at his friend on the bench. "Hey Adam," he called, "I'll race you to the door."

Finally Adam stood up and ambled over to Sam. "Fine, anything to make you stop nagging me. At the count of three."

Adam easily beat Sam to the front door, where he waited, barely out of breath, while Sam ran to catch up, completely winded.

"At least I can still outrun you, Sam," Adam said with the hint of a smile, as they entered the school.

The halls were empty and quiet, and they could hear Mrs. Gold's voice through the door of their classroom. Sam opened the door an inch, and they noticed with relief that their teacher was facing away from the door, busy writing on the blackboard. As silently as cats, they tiptoed to their seats and sat down, keeping a sharp eye on the back of Mrs. Gold's head. But just as they settled in, sharing a smile of relief that they had made it safely, Mrs. Gold spoke from the front of the room.

"So nice of you boys to join us. Perhaps you couldn't hear the bell?"

Sam and Adam gaped at each other.

"Darn," Adam whispered, "that woman has eyes in back of her head!"

"Did you say something?" Mrs. Gold turned to face them. "Since you don't have much regard for time, I think you both can spare me a few minutes after class today."

"Please, Mrs. Gold," Sam said, casting a quick 'I told you so' look at Adam, "my mom is picking me up right after school for my trumpet lesson. Could I stay after school tomorrow instead?"

"I suppose that will have to do," she replied.

Sam sat back in relief, confident that Mrs. Gold would forget his detention by then. She shifted her gaze to Adam.

"Adam, I assume that you are free? No trumpet lessons for you today?"

"No, Mrs. Gold. I can stay." He sighed deeply. What else could go wrong this afternoon? Adam thought glumly.

"Excellent." Mrs. Gold smiled. "Now open your books, please. We were just beginning our unit on chemistry."

Adam snuck a look around the class to see if the other boys on the soccer team were staring at him, but everyone was squinting at the blackboard, trying to decipher the scrawled notes. He breathed a sigh of relief and tried to forget that last horrible moment of the game by focusing on his teacher. Mrs. Gold had been teaching at Rose Park Elementary School for longer than anyone could remember. She looked older than any other teacher, a tiny woman with pure white hair and a pale, wrinkled face. No one knew exactly how old she was. Adam's father had attended Rose Park, and he often told Adam that Mrs. Gold was the oldest teacher at the school back when he was a student. He swore in amazement that she hadn't changed a bit in over thirty years. She was famously strict, but Adam liked the fact that she treated them like grown-ups: no baby talk from her, like some of the younger teachers at Rose Park, who seemed unable to tell the difference between second-graders and fifth-graders.

And, although he would never have admitted this to Sam, Adam liked her because she too was short, almost as short as he was. She was a bit absent-minded, always losing the chalk, her glasses, and her notes, but Adam could not remember a time when she didn't know the answer to a question, no matter how hard, especially when it had to do with science. And science was Adam's favorite subject.

Mrs. Gold resumed her lesson. "Now, where was I? Oh yes, I was just about to ask if anyone could give me a definition of chemistry."

Adam knew the answer, but kept his hand down, reluctant to call attention to himself. Most of the other kids kept their eyes intently on their desks. Only Susie, from her usual spot right in front of the teacher's desk, almost jumped out of her seat as she threw up her hand.

"It's the science of what things are made of."

"Very good, Susie." Mrs. Gold smiled. "That's an excellent definition of chemistry."

Susie looked smug, and Adam had a strong urge to yank her stubby ponytail. But he was already in trouble with Mrs. Gold so he just snuck a look at Sam. They both rolled their eyes.

"And what *are* things made of?" Mrs. Gold asked.

Silence. Even Susie was stumped.

"This desk, for example?" Mrs. Gold patted the top of the desk with her hand. "Or this piece of chalk? Or this meter stick?" Mrs. Gold pointed the stick directly at Sam.

"The stick is made of wood, Mrs. Gold," Sam replied, a bit uncertain if that was the answer she was looking for.

"Well yes, of course it is made of wood, but what is the wood made out of?"

Sam shook his head, hoping that someone else—even Susie—would speak up and pull Mrs. Gold's attention away from him. But the class was silent and still.

Mrs. Gold sighed. "All right, I will give you a hint. If we chop this meter stick into tiny pieces and keep chopping and chopping and chopping until we come down to the smallest pieces of matter we can find, what would we have?"

Adam stared at the meter stick that Mrs. Gold was waving in front of the class, and finally he remembered something he had read in one of the science books his father had given him.

"Atoms?" he whispered, almost to himself.

Mrs. Gold, whose hearing was uncommonly sharp for such an elderly lady, looked him in the eye. "Yes, exactly! Did everyone hear what Adam said?"

Adam squirmed uncomfortably at the attention.

"Speak up, Adam, so everyone can hear."

"Atoms," Adam repeated, still barely above a whisper.

He still was anxious for someone else to grab Mrs. Gold's attention. Fortunately Susie came to his rescue with a frantic wave of her hand.

"Mrs. Gold, I know about atoms. They are too tiny to see, even with a microscope, right?"

"Hey, Adam," Raymond hissed from several seats behind him. "Maybe that explains why you're such a little shrimp: maybe your real name is Atom, not Adam."

Giggles erupted around Raymond, and Adam flushed red. Raymond was the biggest kid in the fifth grade and one of the starters on the soccer team. The only things he seemed to enjoy about school were playing soccer and teasing Adam. Over the years, Adam had become highly skilled at avoiding Raymond, but unfortunately they were in the same class this year.

"Adam the Atom. No wonder you can't kick a soccer ball!"

Adam hunched his shoulders and stared at the floor. This was going to be a long year.

"That's enough, Raymond," Mrs. Gold said. "If you can't be quiet and pay attention, you'll have to go see the principal."

Raymond just smirked and sat back in his chair, twirling a lock of his stringy brown hair around a thick finger.

"Now where was I?" said Mrs. Gold. "Ah, yes, atoms. Some people call atoms the building blocks of the universe because they link together to form all the matter we see in the world. Even though there are thousands and thousands of different substances in the world, there are only 109 kinds of atoms. By combining in different ways, these atoms make up everything we call matter."

"Sort of like Legos?" Sam asked.

"Yes, perfect analogy," Mrs. Gold said, "but much, much smaller."

Mrs. Gold turned and wrote two words on the blackboard: *element* and *compound*. "An element," she said, "is a substance that is made up of only one kind of atom. A compound is made up of two or more different kinds of atoms bonded together."

The students, except for Raymond, who was staring out the window, scribbled furiously in their notebooks.

"Can anyone name an element?" Mrs. Gold asked.

"Water!" Susie called out.

"Good guess, Susie, and once upon a time people did believe that water was an element. But it is actually made of two different elements: hydrogen and oxygen. Any other ideas?"

"Wood?" Sam said, pointing at the meter stick.

"That is another good guess, but wood is also made up of several different elements. We would call it a compound, just like water." Mrs. Gold waited.

Adam knew about the elements from his books at home, but he kept his hand down.

"Here is a clue," Mrs. Gold said finally. "Many elements are metals."

"Gold?" Susie sounded excited.

"Yes!" Mrs. Gold smiled.

Now the students didn't hesitate.

"Silver."

"Copper."

"Iron."

Mrs. Gold practically beamed. "Yes, yes, yes. Excellent. Now here is a harder question: some elements are gases. Can you think of one?"

"Yeah." Raymond laughed, finally attentive. "Farts. Hey Adam the Atom, passed any gas lately?"

The class erupted in laughter as Adam cringed.

"Why, Raymond," Mrs. Gold said, silencing the class with a glare, "I'm glad you were paying attention to my question, but a fart would be a compound. Any other ideas?"

Raymond slumped back in his seat in silence.

"Adam, you look like you have an idea."

Adam looked up at Mrs. Gold and wondered how she knew what he was thinking about. "Well," he said quietly, "I think oxygen is a gas."

"Absolutely correct," said Mrs. Gold, her head bobbing up and down enthusiastically. "Can you think of any others?"

Adam was reluctant to reveal how much he knew, fearing that it would be one more reason for Raymond to make fun of him, but Mrs. Gold would not take her eyes off him. "Nitrogen and helium," he finally said.

Mrs. Gold nodded her head vigorously. "Good job, Adam."

"Good job, Adam the Atom," Raymond mimicked from the back.

Mrs. Gold ignored him, but Adam felt his face grow hot.

"They use helium in balloons, don't they, Mrs. Gold?" Sarah asked from the front of the room, where she sat next to Susie. "Yes, Sarah, and that is why helium balloons float: Helium is lighter than air."

"It also makes you talk funny if you breathe it," Sam added, remembering a trick he learned at a birthday party.

Then Mrs. Gold pointed to a chart on the wall. "This chart will be our guide as we study elements and atoms. It is called the Periodic Table, and it was invented over a hundred years ago by a Russian scientist." She wrote *Dmitri Mendeleev* on the blackboard. "That's pronounced Di-mee-tree Men-de-lay-eff, and I will expect you all to remember his name."

The students scribbled in their notebooks. Adam glanced at the chart, which looked like an irregular rectangle divided into columns and rows.

"The Periodic Table lists all the elements in order of something called atomic number," Mrs. Gold continued, pointing to one of the boxes on the chart with some numbers and letters. "It has to do with protons and neutrons and electrons, but don't worry about that yet," she said. "We'll get to it later this week."

"All the elements belong to 'families,' just like people," Mrs. Gold said quickly, looking at the clock. "And you can tell what family they are in by looking at this table. All the elements in a column—" She ran her finger up and down the table.—"have similar properties, and …"

"Hey, Adam the Atom, what family are you in?" Raymond interrupted.

Several students giggled, but Mrs. Gold's cold stare quieted the class, and even Raymond stopped smirking. She continued, "Some of the families have names, like the halogens, here in column number seven, or the noble gases, in the last column in the table."

"Why are they called noble, Mrs. Gold?" Susie asked, but the bell rang before Mrs. Gold could answer.

"We'll talk about that tomorrow," she called out as the students closed their notebooks and grabbed their backpacks.

Adam sat quietly while his classmates filed out of the room. Sam gave him a sympathetic glance as he hurried off to his trumpet lesson, and Susie flounced out with her little crew of girlfriends.

"See ya later, Adam the Atom," Raymond jeered as he raced out to meet his buddies in the hall.

Adam waited in the empty room for Mrs. Gold to speak to him, but she sat down at the desk and busied herself with some papers. He knew enough not to interrupt her, so he put his head down on his desk to wait. It had been a long day.

Chapter Two

"OK, Adam, come on up here."

Adam jerked himself upright. Had he fallen asleep? The room was eerily quiet and empty as he shuffled over to Mrs. Gold's desk. Her voice was kind, but Adam didn't like the way she was staring at him. He dreaded what was coming, but at the same time, he was impatient to get it over with. He stood quietly, staring at the carpet.

"Tough soccer game today. Is that why you were late?"

Adam looked up sharply in surprise. He didn't think she paid any attention to what the kids did during recess. Mrs. Gold smiled at his puzzled expression.

"Oh, I like to watch your games from my window. You're very fast aren't you, Adam? Too bad you don't get to play more often."

Adam flushed. Did *everyone* at Rose Park know that he was a bench warmer? "Mrs. Gold," he said, "I am really sorry we were late today, and it was all my fault. Sam stayed back to talk to me after the game. I promise we won't do it again. Do you want me to clean the blackboard or something?"

Instead of answering, Mrs. Gold walked over to the window, where she gazed at the empty yard, seemingly lost in thought. Adam waited, shifting back and forth on his feet, afraid to interrupt her. Finally she spoke.

"You like studying chemistry, don't you, Adam?"

He nodded silently.

"Yes, I think you are just the boy for the job," she said.

"What job, Mrs. Gold? Do you want me to clean the erasers?"

"The erasers? Oh goodness, Adam, what a silly thought," she said with a small laugh.

"But what kind of job would you like me to do?"

"Ah, something much more important than blackboards and erasers. Something that has to do with chemistry."

"Chemistry?" Adam asked. Maybe she wanted him to help her prepare an experiment for the class.

"Yes, something to do with the elements."

Adam listened closely, curious about the turn of the conversation.

"You see, Adam, I've been worried about something all day," Mrs. Gold said, turning to face him. Her lips were pressed together, and her forehead wrinkled in a tiny frown. "I have a serious problem to solve, and I believe that you may be the only one who can help."

"Me?" Adam sputtered. "But really, Mrs. Gold I don't know much chemistry at all."

"Now don't be nervous, Adam. Let's sit down. I have a lot to explain."

Mrs. Gold sat down in one of the student chairs, and she motioned Adam to sit down facing her. Seated like this, her face was exactly the same height as his, and she leaned in so close he could hear her breathing. He noticed the little lines around her eyes and the wisps of gray hair that fell onto her face. Adam wanted to back away, but he found that his eyes were locked onto hers.

"Have you ever heard of alchemy?" she asked.

Adam wasn't sure he had heard her correctly. "Alchemy?"

"Alchemy," she repeated. "It was an ancient and powerful art, and most modern chemists have forgotten all about it."

"Was it like magic?" Adam asked.

If Mrs. Gold wasn't going to talk about his punishment, he certainly wasn't going to raise the topic. He was happy to let her ramble on. Mrs. Gold leaned back in her chair, and Adam watched her closely as she looked away from him and off into the distance.

"Long before the science of modern chemistry, alchemists tried to figure out what matter was made of and how to control the different elements. Unfortunately, too many alchemists thought that they could turn lead into gold and wasted their lives trying to become rich. So they got a bad reputation, and people now think of them as magicians or con men." Mrs. Gold's eyes turned back to Adam, and her voice dropped to a whisper. "But the alchemists knew a lot more about the chemical elements than anyone realizes, and their knowledge was carefully passed on to new generations of alchemists who must work in secret."

Adam squirmed uncomfortably in his seat. Alchemy sounded like voodoo. But he was unable to pull his eyes away from hers.

"I know this sounds crazy, Adam, but I need you to know the truth." She leaned so close he could feel her breath. "Teaching at Rose Park Elementary School is just a hobby for me." Mrs. Gold hesitated, and then she pressed her lips together in determination. "My real work is alchemy."

Adam was too stunned to reply. He stood up and backed away from Mrs. Gold, inching toward the door. Was she crazy? Alchemy? He looked out to the hall, wondering if anyone would hear him if he called for help. He was almost at the door when Mrs. Gold stood up.

"Please, Adam. You really have to believe me. I need your help!"

Adam hesitated. She was talking nonsense, but she was still his teacher, one of the best he had had at Rose Park. How he could he be afraid of such a kind little old woman? He approached her cautiously, and she smiled gently as he took his seat again.

Mrs. Gold's voice was tense. "I received an urgent message today from the Council of Alchemists. There is a crisis with the element oxygen."

"Oxygen?" he asked. "Like the stuff we breathe?"

Mrs. Gold sighed. "Yes, exactly so. Without it, no one can live— not people nor animals, not even fish. Do you understand?"

Adam nodded his head.

"Remember the lesson in class today?" she asked. "About how all the elements are made up of very tiny atoms—much, much smaller than you are?"

Adam flushed, remembering Raymond's taunt in class.

"Before these atoms can go out into the world and do their jobs, they must learn the properties of their element," Mrs. Gold continued. "Every element is unique, with an important job to do, and it is essential that the atoms be carefully instructed so they know how to behave, what reactions to participate in, and how to interact with other elements. So, of course, they need to go to school."

Adam's eyes widened, and he nodded his head.

"We call this special school the Periodic School for Elements. Naturally it doesn't look at all like Rose Park Elementary School; that wouldn't make any sense, would it?" Mrs. Gold smiled at Adam, and he forced himself to smile back and nod his head. "No, this school looks just like the periodic table we were studying in class today." She pointed toward the chart on the wall. "The one that Mendeleev put together."

Adam looked at the periodic table, remembering the lesson from the morning. He nodded silently, staring at the colorful chart with its strange symbols and numbers.

"There are only a handful of alchemists left in the world," Mrs. Gold continued, "and we have different jobs—none of which involves making gold, I might add." She smiled at her own joke. Adam forced his lips into a tight smile in return. "My job is to keep an eye on the Periodic School and make sure that all the atoms make a smooth transition to our own world when they are fully trained. The teachers there keep me informed when a new batch of atoms will be ready. Do you understand, Adam?"

"Not really," he whispered.

"That's okay. I know this is hard to accept, but please believe me: my job is really important. The message I received came from the oxygen teacher. One of his young pupils is missing! He never came back to his room after recess. You might know something about that."

Mrs. Gold peered at him over her glasses, and Adam shifted uncomfortably remembering how Sam had to practically drag him back to class after recess. He nodded.

"The oxygen teacher assumes that something happened to the young atom—Ollie is his name. But unfortunately none of Ollie's friends know what. The last time they saw him, he was talking to some of the precious metals."

"Precious metals," said Adam, caught up in the story despite himself. "You mean like gold?"

"Yes, yes. That's right! You do know your chemistry. Oh, I knew you were the right boy for this job!" Mrs. Gold smiled warmly at Adam. "But that's not the worst of it. There are some important rules at the Periodic School, and one rule states that a teacher cannot continue to instruct a class unless all the students are present. So, until this atom is found and returns to his class, the oxygen teacher can't do his job."

"So?" Adam asked, curious despite himself.

"Well, don't you see?" Mrs. Gold asked. "If the teacher can't train the oxygen atoms to do their jobs in the world, none of them will graduate. We need a new supply of atoms from the Periodic School every day, and if the oxygen teacher can't finish training the atoms, we will run out of oxygen on earth!"

Mrs. Gold's voice had gotten higher and shriller, and she now stood up with her hands on her hips, looking at Adam. He stared at her in disbelief. If there were no oxygen atoms, then no one would be able to breathe, which meant everyone would die. The situation was so outrageous that Adam had a sudden thought: Maybe he was dreaming. Maybe he had dozed off in class just before the bell rang. He rubbed his eyes and pinched his arm, but when he opened his eyes, Mrs. Gold was still looking at him earnestly.

"I hope you understand the seriousness of the problem," Mrs. Gold said. "And that is why I need your help. You need to go to the

Periodic School, learn what happened to this runaway atom, find him, and convince him to go back to his class."

Adam sat frozen in his chair, staring at Mrs. Gold. He searched her face for a hint of a smile, thinking that any moment she would laugh with him about her excellent joke, but there was no hint of a smile on her face. She was deadly serious.

"Mrs. Gold," he stammered hesitantly. "You're joking, right? You're just pulling my leg to see if I was paying attention during our chemistry lesson."

Mrs. Gold shook her head. "I have never been more serious, Adam. And I am more certain than ever that you are the perfect person to find Ollie and prevent a terrible catastrophe."

CHAPTER THREE

Adam stood, his heart beating hard against his chest. Mrs. Gold had obviously gone over the edge. And he was furious with himself. If he hadn't missed that last shot in the soccer game, he wouldn't have been late from recess, and he could have escaped this whole meeting. He thought frantically about how to get away without hurting her feelings, but before he could say anything, she went over to her desk and took out a small canvas bag.

"Ah, here it is," she said, pulling out a white stone about the size of a golf ball. "Come over here, Adam. I need to show you the philosopher's stone."

Adam walked slowly and deliberately to her desk. She held out the stone for him to see. It looked like a plain rock, only smoother and completely white. He couldn't figure out why Mrs. Gold was handling it as if it were made of crystal.

"The philosopher's stone," she explained, "is the secret magical tool of the alchemists. For centuries, alchemists searched the world for this stone because they believed it would turn lead into gold. Silly idea."

Adam looked back and forth between Mrs. Gold and the stone, his mind a jumble.

"Of course you can't change lead to gold." Mrs. Gold leaned her face right up to Adam's. She whispered, "But the philosopher's stone can do something even more amazing: it is the key into the Periodic School of the Elements. I was entrusted with this stone when I was given the job of watching over the school. I am too old to use it anymore, or I would find that rascal oxygen atom myself. You have to be young and nimble to travel by means of the philosopher's stone." Mrs. Gold put her hand on Adam's shoulder. "That means that you, Adam, are the perfect person for this mission. I am sending you inside the Periodic School."

Adam stared at Mrs. Gold in disbelief.

"Now here is the plan," Mrs. Gold continued. "I am going to trust you with the philosopher's stone, but you need to be careful not to lose it, or else you won't be able to get out of the school and back home. Ollie is hiding somewhere in the school, and your job is to find him and get him back to his own classroom. A good start would be to learn what happened to him during recess. I will give you a copy of the periodic table to help you find your way around the school. Use it like a map. It won't be hard. All the rooms are numbered."

Adam looked at the periodic table on the wall.

"You can see that each element has its own atomic number," she said, "and those are the same numbers you will see on the doors of each classroom."

Adam looked back at the philosopher's stone in Mrs. Gold hand.

"This won't be easy," she continued. "The Periodic School has lots of places where a young oxygen atom could hide. You don't have much time. Remember, if you don't get Ollie back where he belongs by the end of the day, our world will run out of oxygen and ..." Her voice trailed off, as if she couldn't bear to finish the sentence.

Adam's mind was racing. How could he get out of this? Darned Sam and his trumpet lesson. Why hadn't he thought of that? Maybe he could explain that he had to get home to watch his little sister. She was actually at ballet, but Mrs. Gold wouldn't know that.

Then he had a comforting thought. All he had to do was humor her by taking this little stone and pretending to go along with her plan. Since there was obviously no such thing as a philosopher's stone, let alone a Periodic School for Elements, in no time at all he could be safely at home. Adam gave Mrs. Gold his most reassuring smile.

"Do I just hold the stone?" he asked.

"Oh no," she replied. "You need to recite the correct verse. There is one verse to get in and another to get out. Now pay close attention, or, as I said, you'll be stuck forever in the Periodic School. To enter the school, you say:

> Iron, cobalt, nickel, tin,
> Mendeleev, let me in."

Adam repeated the verse, and Mrs. Gold nodded approval.

"Now, when it is time to come home, you hold the stone and say:

> Argon, neon, helium,
> Mendeleev, take me home."

Mrs. Gold listened closely as Adam recited the verse. "Perfect," she said, "but in case you have trouble remembering this verse when it is time to come home, just think of the noble gases."

Adam nodded his head. It wasn't worth explaining to Mrs. Gold that he didn't know what a noble gas was.

"Now take this copy of the periodic table. Remember: it is your map of the school."

Adam put the table in his pocket and took the philosopher's stone from Mrs. Gold.

"As soon as you recite the verse, you will shrink to the size of an atom, and you will be transported to the Periodic School of Elements," she said. "I have arranged it so you will land just outside the school—it is safer that way, since otherwise I can't be sure what room you would end up in. I don't want you to accidentally end up with one of the radioactive elements, like radium or uranium, or you might get too sick to look for Ollie."

"Radioactive?" Adam asked.

"Oh, right," Mrs. Gold replied. "We haven't gotten to that part of the lesson yet, have we?"

Adam shook his head.

"Well, you don't need to understand how it works, but radioactive elements give off tiny alpha and beta particles, and sometimes these particles can make you sick."

"What do you mean, sick? How sick?" Adam couldn't help sounding worried.

"Oh my," Mrs. Gold said quickly. "I didn't mean to upset you. I'll fix it so you can hear the radioactive elements giving off particles so the sound will warn you to stay away. Now remember, Adam. I won't be able to help you once you are inside the school, so the fate of the world is on your shoulders." She stepped back. "Good luck!"

Adam sighed. Might as well get this little charade over with. Maybe Mrs. Gold would return to her normal self tomorrow. He wondered if he should tell his mother about this conversation, but he didn't want to get Mrs. Gold into trouble. After all, until this conversation, he considered himself lucky to have her for a teacher.

Mrs. Gold motioned for Adam to stand in the center of the room. He held the white stone tightly in his hand and recited:

> "Iron, cobalt, nickel, tin,
> Mendeleev, let me in."

At first nothing happened, and Adam looked over at Mrs. Gold, who had backed toward the wall. But then he noticed that the light overhead had gotten much brighter. Suddenly the walls of the classroom were spinning around him. The blackboard and bulletin boards were a blur, and he felt as if he were about to fall. He gripped the philosopher's stone tightly in his fist. Suddenly he was floating off the ground, and as he watched, Mrs. Gold got bigger and bigger until she blended into the swirling cloud of white light.

He could feel his heart pounding quickly against his chest. He was on the verge of panic. He squeezed his eyes shut, but the light came through and he could still feel himself spinning. He couldn't breathe. He couldn't scream. He couldn't hear anything but a whooshing noise as he spun faster and faster. The pressure on his head was intense.

Just when he thought he couldn't take anymore, the pressure eased and he felt himself slowing down. The light dimmed, and he started to fall. He braced himself for hitting the ground, but somehow he drifted down slowly and landed on something soft. It took him a few seconds to gather the courage to open his eyes.

Adam was lying on something that looked like grass, and he could feel the sun shining overhead. He sat up slowly. Nothing hurt, thank goodness, but he was shaking. He looked around and saw that he was on the lawn of a large brick building.

"Mrs. Gold," he shouted. "Where are you? What's going on?"

But there was no answer. There was no sign of Mrs. Gold anywhere. In fact, there was no sign of anyone at all. Adam jumped to his feet and looked around in growing panic. All he saw was an endless lawn of grass and the one building. There was no sidewalk, no cars, no school buses, nothing. His stomach was in a knot. He certainly wasn't at Rose Park Elementary School anymore.

Resisting the urge to panic, he pulled the periodic table from his pocket and studied the building in front of him. It was shaped exactly like the table. He thought about Mrs. Gold's instructions to him. Was it possible that she *was* an alchemist? That he was now in atom-land? There didn't seem to be any other explanation for what had happened to him, and no one was answering his calls.

His only choice was to go inside the school and investigate. Adam took several deep breaths to calm down, put the philosopher's stone carefully into his pocket, and entered the front door.

CHAPTER FOUR

Adam found himself on the first floor of the school. The floor and walls were completely white and smooth, and, unlike in his own school, all the rooms were on the same side of the hall. He scanned the hallway, but it was completely deserted.

A sign on the wall said "Row 7." He was confused for a moment, since he was sure he had come in on the ground floor. He checked the periodic table that Mrs. Gold had given him and realized that the number made sense. On the table, the highest floor was Row 1, and the bottom floor was Row 7. It was the opposite of his school, where the lowest floor was number one.

Each door was marked with a square sign that listed two numbers, the name of an element and a symbol that looked like a short version of the name. Adam looked back and forth between the periodic table and the hallway. The squares on the doors were exactly the same as the squares on the periodic table. He did not want to believe what he was seeing, but it looked like Mrs. Gold had been telling the truth. How else could he explain the bizarre events of the morning? Adam had shrunk to the size of an atom, and he was inside the Periodic School of Elements! But if Mrs. Gold had been telling the truth about being an alchemist and the Periodic School for the elements really existed, then she must also have been telling the truth about Ollie.

Somewhere in this building, an oxygen atom was hiding, and if Adam did not find him, the world would run out of oxygen. Adam shuddered.

The names on the doors were strange and meant nothing to him: Meitnerium, Hassium, Bohrium, Seaborgium. Finally he came to a name that sounded familiar. He studied the sign on the door:

88
Ra
Radium
226.0

Maybe this was a good place to look for someone who could help him. As he reached for the doorknob, he heard lots of rattling noises, as if a whole bunch of kids were throwing ping-pong balls against the walls. Weird, he thought. He paused with his hand on the doorknob. Why did the name radium sound so familiar? Suddenly it came to him: It was one of the elements Mrs. Gold had said was radioactive. Those pinging noises must be the alpha and beta particles she had told him about. The ones that would make him sick. He let go of the doorknob as if it were hot and backed away from the door. He stopped and listened at the door right next to Radium—it said Francium—and he heard that same pinging noise. Adam pulled the table out of his pocket and looked carefully at the names of elements, searching for something that looked familiar. One name caught his eye: Gold. That should be safe, he thought. He noted its location on the map and bounded up the stairs two at a time.

On Row 6, Adam again saw a long white hall with rooms that corresponded to the boxes on the periodic table. He walked past Barium, Tungsten, Osmium, and Platinum and stopped in front of the door marked number 79.

```
79
Au
Gold
197.0
```

Adam didn't know what the numbers or symbol Au meant, but saw what he was looking for: the word gold. He knew that gold was not radioactive or dangerous—it couldn't be if it was used for jewelry. And then Adam remembered something else that Mrs. Gold had told him. The last time Ollie was seen, he was talking to some precious metals. Well, you don't get more precious than gold, he said to himself as he opened the door.

Adam stared in astonishment at the strange sight that greeted him. The room looked like a regular classroom, but the students at the desks did not look like any children he had ever seen. They had huge heads, tiny bodies, and, instead of hair, they had what looked like beads spinning around their heads. The students were the color of gold. The teacher—who looked just like the students, only older— stood at the front of the class writing on the blackboard: *Chemical and Physical Properties of Gold*. Adam crouched down in the back of the room so he could observe for a while without being noticed.

The gold atoms were paying no attention to the teacher. Instead, they were all holding mirrors and gazing raptly at their lustrous shiny surfaces. They were too busy preening in front of their mirrors to notice Adam. Finally the teacher rapped his ruler on the desk to get their attention.

Reluctantly the students put down their mirrors.

"Good morning class," the teacher said. "As one of the most important and valuable of all elements, we gold atoms must always set an example for other elements by knowing our lessons perfectly."

The students all beamed at each other, and began to recite the lesson that they had carefully memorized:

We are the perfect element
So lovely to behold.
The ancients named us aurum.
But you can call us gold.

In olden days gold filled the vaults
Of emperors and kings.
Today we're found as jewelry,
From necklaces to rings.

Our lustrous shine will never fade,
No matter what you do.
Drop us in an acid bath,
We come out good as new.

We're very heavy, very dense.
And crazy as it sounds
A basketball, if solid gold,
Would weigh 300 pounds.

Well, that explained their haughty manner, thought Adam. He didn't know much about the properties of gold they were learning, but he did know that anything made of gold cost a lot of money. The students in this room must be gold atoms, just like Mrs. Gold had talked about in his class this afternoon. They were learning their lessons so they would remember all the properties of the element gold when it was time for them to leave school.

So far everything Mrs. Gold had told him was true. That meant that somewhere in this Periodic School an oxygen atom named Ollie was hiding. And it was up to Adam to find him. He stood up and slowly approached one of the gold atoms.

"Excuse me," he said softly.

No response. The gold atom did not even turn his head in Adam's direction.

"Excuse me," Adam said more loudly.

Still no response. Finally Adam gingerly tapped the gold atom on the back. The atom nearly jumped out of his seat.

"What do you think you're doing in here?" He glared at Adam. "You obviously don't belong with us—you don't shine at all!"

"Shh," Adam said, looking nervously toward the front of the room to see if teacher had noticed him.

Fortunately, the teacher had picked up his own mirror and was so completely absorbed in admiring his reflection that he was unaware of Adam. The gold atom regarded Adam with distaste.

"I've never seen anyone as weird-looking as you. What kind of atom are you, anyway?"

Adam was shocked by his rudeness; the gold atom was almost as nasty as Raymond. Adam forced himself to be polite.

"Please excuse me," Adam said to the gold atom. "I did not mean to startle you, but I am not an atom at all, just a boy from ..."

"Boy? What's a boy? How did you get here?"

"Please," Adam said, "I don't really have time to explain. I was sent to find Ollie—an oxygen atom. I thought he might be hiding here in the gold room."

"Oxygen! What would an oxygen atom be doing here?" the gold atom huffed. "Oxygen isn't even a metal, let alone a precious metal."

Another gold atom who was listening started to laugh. "Oxygen, what an absurd idea! We would never let an oxygen in our room!"

But then a third gold atom interrupted: "Wait a second," he said, "I did see an oxygen atom at recess today. Scrawny little fellow, kind of blue in the face. He was all alone. I wondered what he was doing, hanging around the metals."

"Yes, yes," Adam said breathlessly. "That must have been Ollie. Did you talk to him?"

"Of course not! What are you thinking? I'm a gold atom, not some flighty gas. Why on earth would I ever talk to an oxygen atom?"

"But something happened at recess," Adam persisted. "And now Ollie is missing. Can't you remember anything that happened out there today?"

Finally the gold atom put down his mirror and closed his eyes. The seconds ticked by, and the gold atom did not move. Adam feared he might have fallen asleep. Suddenly he opened his eyes and then gestured for Adam to come closer.

"Shh," the gold atom whispered. "I don't want my friends to know that I had anything to do with an oxygen atom—what's his name again?"

"Ollie."

"Right. Ollie. Well, after the gold atoms chased him away at recess, I saw him slink over toward a group of silver atoms."

Adam looked at him, puzzled. "Why did you chase him away?"

"Are you a complete idiot?" said the gold atom. "Gold atoms are the most beautiful, the most valuable element in the school, and we stick to ourselves. We don't like to bond with other elements. What other element could possibly be up to our standard?"

Adam's face was stuck in a tight smile. He couldn't believe how stuck up and self-centered these gold atoms were. "But then what happened when Ollie went over to the silver atoms?"

"How should I know? I think I've helped you out quite enough already."

With that, the gold atom grabbed his mirror and was soon lost in admiration for his shiny reflection. Adam could see that there was no point in trying to get any more information here; he was lucky to have gotten even one small hint. Adam breathed a sigh of relief once he was back out in the hall. He knew what it was like to be picked on by kids who felt superior to everyone else, and he felt a pang of sympathy for Ollie, wherever he might be hiding.

CHAPTER FIVE

"Sounds like my next step is to find the silver atoms," Adam said to himself. He pulled out the periodic table Mrs. Gold had given him and found the box that contained the name Silver. He had no trouble locating the right place. It was on Row 5, right above the room for gold.

Racing down the hall, Adam was surprised to see an atom standing just outside the door.

```
47
Ag
Silver
107.9
```

Up close, Adam could see that he was mostly the color of the silver he had seen at home and shiny, just like the gold atoms. But he had black splotches all over his body. He, too, had beads swirling around his head. The silver atom did not notice Adam because he was furiously polishing himself with a cloth.

"Have you seen an oxygen atom today?" Adam asked.

The silver atom jumped at the sound of Adam's voice. "Of course I have," the silver atom answered angrily. "Why do you think I am all covered in tarnish?"

"Tarnish?"

"It's kind of like rust," said the silver atom impatiently, "and it happens when I come into contact with oxygen. I've been out here scrubbing since recess, and I've got to get this tarnish off or else I am going to get in trouble with my teacher. She insists that we all be perfectly clean for class."

Adam watched in fascination as the silver atom scrubbed off the black coating to reveal a shiny surface underneath.

"Where exactly did you see this oxygen atom?" Adam asked. "And when?"

"Didn't I already say that it was at recess?" the silver atom snapped. "Why are you asking me all these questions?" The silver atom stopped polishing and looked more closely at Adam. "Who are you anyway? What is your element name? I don't recognize you."

"My name is Adam, and …"

"Atom," said the silver. "Of course you're an atom. We're all atoms. But where are your electrons?"

"Not atom, *Adam*," Adam said. "I'm a boy, not an element. And what are electrons anyway?"

The silver atom stared suspiciously at Adam. "These are electrons, dummy," he said, pointing to the beads around his head. "We all have electrons—protons and neutrons, too, but you can't see those— they're deep inside."

Adam vaguely remembered Mrs. Gold mentioning protons, neutrons, and electrons this afternoon, but she hadn't had time to explain. And there was no time now to ask for a chemistry lesson.

"Listen," said Adam. "I really need your help. That oxygen atom you saw is named Ollie, and he never came back to his own class after recess."

"What?" said the silver atom. "That's impossible. Every atom knows where it belongs in the Periodic School. If elements wandered around, who knows what dangerous reactions could happen. Especially with oxygen. Man, those guys are reactive!"

"What do you mean?" Adam felt lost and wished Mrs. Gold had had time to teach him more chemistry before sending him on this mission.

"Reactions—you know, like when atoms bond together to form new substances. Sometimes things can get really hot when they combine."

"Is that what happens when you get too close to oxygen?" Adam asked.

The silver atom laughed. "You really are stupid, you know."

Adam winced. He was used to being called short, but never stupid.

"We don't explode or anything like that with oxygen," the silver atom said. "We just tarnish. But that's bad enough. Look how ugly I look!" And with that he started rubbing himself again with his polishing cloth.

"Stop, please," Adam pleaded with the silver atom. "You haven't heard the worst of it."

"How could it be worse?" asked the silver atom.

"Mrs. Gold told me that, without Ollie, his teacher can't finish training the oxygen atoms."

"Who's Mrs. Gold?" the silver atom asked. "Is she one of the gold atoms?"

"No, no," Adam replied impatiently "She's not an element either. She's my teacher!"

Now it was the silver atom's turn to look confused. "But how is she teaching your class if you're here in the Periodic School instead of where you belong?"

This is getting nowhere, thought Adam, struggling to remain calm.

"Please, I need to find Ollie and get him back to his class. If I don't, the oxygen atoms won't finish learning their properties, and they won't graduate and be sent off to do their jobs in my world. That means there won't be any more oxygen for people to breathe. Do you know what that means?"

The silver atom shook his head.

"It means that everyone will die!" Adam's voice shook with emotion.

The silver atom finally stopped polishing himself and looked more closely at this Adam who wasn't an atom. "And dying—it's a bad thing, huh?"

Adam couldn't speak for the moment and just nodded.

"Well, then, let me think. It seems to me that after I chased Ollie away, he headed off to the swings, where the copper atoms were playing. We are cousins, you know. Same family."

"Family?"

Once again the silver atom shook his head at Adam's ignorance. "The precious metal family. Don't you know anything about chemistry?"

Adam sighed. He had started the day thinking he knew a lot about chemistry, but he was quickly finding out how much more he needed to learn. He vaguely remembered Mrs. Gold talking about element families in class. He pulled the periodic table out of his pocket, reaching deep inside to make sure the philosopher's stone was still safe.

"Let's see. I think Mrs. Gold said that chemical families were all in the same column on the chart. Is that right?" Adam asked, hoping he didn't sound too dumb.

The silver atom rolled his eyes. "Well, duh. Everyone knows that."

Adam ignored the sarcasm and plunged ahead. "So maybe the copper atoms would be able to tell me what happened during recess?"

"Maybe," said the silver atom, "but they don't like oxygen any more than I do."

"Thanks for your help," Adam called, as he took off at full speed toward the stairs.

The silver atom paid no attention, returning to the task of cleaning off his tarnish.

CHAPTER SIX

Adam quickly located the copper room on Row 4. It was easy to find because it was right on top of the room for silver. The room was labeled:

```
29
Cu
Copper
63.55
```

Adam stepped inside and noticed that the atoms looked a little bit like the gold atoms, but smaller and not as shiny. They were the color of brand new pennies. They had lots of those bead-like electrons swirling around their heads, but not nearly as many as the gold atoms. Adam guessed there were around twenty or thirty electrons for each atom, but he couldn't count them because they whizzed around so fast they formed a kind of cloud.

The teacher was leading a lesson, so Adam couldn't ask anyone about Ollie. He listened to the students recite in unison.

Like gold and silver, copper's used
To make fine jewelry.
Because we three are so alike,
We're called a family.

We tarnish just like silver,
Which turns our surface green.
But rub us with some polish
And we'll be shiny clean.

Copper's used in batteries,
Electric wire and sockets.
It's also found in pots and pans,
And pennies in your pockets.

Adam scanned the room, not knowing exactly what he was looking for, but then he noticed that one of the copper atoms had a green spot on her back. He knew from the lesson that this was tarnish, just like the stuff he saw on the silver atom. If copper had similar properties to silver—which would make sense if they were in the same family—then that meant that this copper atom had been near Ollie. The copper atom clearly did not know about the green spot, since she was happily reciting her lesson with the rest of the class.

Tiptoeing up to the copper atom, Adam whispered as quietly as he could, "Excuse me, but could you tell me how you got that green spot on your back?"

The copper atom jumped out of her seat and screamed—not the result that Adam had hoped for. Naturally, the teacher stopped the lesson, and glared at both of them.

"What's the matter, Connie?" he asked. "You are interrupting my lesson!"

Connie had backed away from Adam, but she was still screaming. And now all the other copper atoms were staring at him.

Adam had to yell over her voice. "I am so sorry to disturb your class, sir, but I need to find out what happened to an oxygen atom named Ollie at recess today. You see, he is missing and ..."

"You don't need to say another word," responded the teacher, "a missing atom is a serious problem, especially oxygen. And why do you think Connie can help you?"

"I noticed a small green spot on her back and ..."

With that Connie spun around, trying desperately to see her own back, and some of her friends jumped out of their seats to help her. They formed a little knot around her and shook their heads in sympathy. One of them pulled out a cloth and began to wipe at the tarnish. Connie had finally stopped screaming, but she was trembling. Her friends murmured cooing noises of comfort.

"Girls," Adam muttered to himself.

"Connie, I want to you to step outside the class and talk to this, this ... What kind of element are you, anyway?"

"Not an element, sir. I am just a boy."

"Boron, did you say? You don't look like boron."

"No, not boron: boy. I'm a boy."

"Never heard of it. Are you one of those newfangled man-made transuranium elements?"

Adam had no idea what the teacher was talking about, so he repeated, "No sir, just a boy," and hurried out of the class to wait for Connie.

She finally appeared, much subdued and red-eyed from the trauma in the classroom. She crossed her arms angrily in front of her.

"Well, now that you've got me in trouble, what do you want?"

Adam took a moment to check and see that her tarnish had been cleaned off. "You look very clean and shiny now," he said, hoping to appease her.

"No thanks to you," she huffed. "I have friends who care about me—something I bet you wouldn't know about. Who would want to hang out with a weird-looking atom like you?"

Once again Adam winced, thinking that atoms could be just as mean as some of the kids in his school. He wished Sam were here to help him and so Adam could show this uppity atom that he did in fact have friends. But he held his temper.

"I am so sorry that I startled you just now, but I really have to find Ollie. My own world is depending on me." Adam prepared to explain the situation all over again, but Connie didn't seem interested.

"I don't know why anyone would want to find a stupid oxygen atom, anyway. Especially one who doesn't know his place."

"What do you mean?" Adam asked eagerly.

"He's a gas, for goodness sake," Connie said. "And he is always trying to bond with the other elements, whether they want to or not." She paused at the puzzled look on Adam's face. "You know what bonding is, don't you?"

Adam felt her distain, and he flushed with embarrassment at his own ignorance. These atoms had no patience.

"Bonding is when atoms trade or share electrons to form compounds," she recited in a sing-song voice. Clearly this was one of the more elementary lessons they teach at the Periodic School, Adam realized.

"Is bonding bad?" asked Adam in the most polite voice he could muster.

Connie made no effort to conceal her frustration with Adam. "Not always," she replied, "but we metals prefer to bond with ourselves so we don't lose our bright, shiny surfaces. You've seen what happens when oxygen gets too close: we *rust*." Connie shivered with disgust as she said the last word.

"So what happened at recess today?" Adam continued, although he was beginning to form his own guess.

"Well, I was talking with my two best friends, Carol and Callie, about whether it was better to go out with a zinc atom and make brass or a tin atom and make bronze. Carol was asked out on a date by Ziggy, which is nice because his classroom is right next door to ours and his atomic number is a nice round thirty. But we think it is definitely more classy to wait and see if Tim will ask her out also, because that way they can make some beautiful bronze together, and you know that bronze is one of the most important alloys in the whole world. It is stronger than iron and you can use it to make statues and bells. But then again, some people think that brass is also attractive and useful, especially if you like jazz music and trumpets and trombones and stuff like that—"

"Please, Connie," Adam interrupted, looking impatiently at his watch. "What about Ollie?"

Connie rolled her eyes. "Fine. Well, we were so deep into our discussion that we didn't notice this scrawny blue oxygen atom until he was right next to us, and then ..."

"Yes?" Adam could barely contain his impatience.

"We screamed! We jumped up and started screaming—anything to get him to leave us alone."

"Can you remember what you said? Please try," Adam pleaded.

Connie screwed up her face in concentration. "Rust Rat. We called him a dirty rust rat."

"That's so mean," Adam said, recoiling. "Ollie can't help who he is."

"Well, it's true. We told him to get away from us. 'No one wants to bond with you,' we said."

Adam struggled to control his anger—how could Connie and her friends be so cruel? He had never even met Ollie, but he felt sorry for him. This was far worse than having Raymond call Adam a shrimp or an atom. No wonder Ollie ran away.

"Where did Ollie go after you yelled at him?" Adam asked, barely managing to keep his voice even.

Connie thought for a few seconds. "He ran back over to where the gases were playing, where he belongs," she said finally.

"But Ollie did not show up in his own class after recess," Adam told her. "Where else could he have gone?"

"Maybe you should check some of the halogens. They're over-reactive gases, just like oxygen." She paused at the puzzled look on Adam's face. "Oh right, I forgot, you don't know much about the elements, do you?" She rolled her eyes in derision. "The halogen gases are fluorine and chlorine. They occupy the family right next to oxygen. That's where I would look, if I were you, not that I would waste any time looking for a rust rat named Ollie."

And with that, Connie flounced back to her classroom and slammed the door behind her.

CHAPTER SEVEN

Adam stood for a moment outside the door to the copper room, breathing deeply, trying to calm down. He wanted to throttle Connie, but that was as useless a thought as wanting to throttle Raymond. So he took the periodic table out of his pocket, once again checking to make sure the philosopher's stone was safe, and located the boxes for fluorine and chlorine. Chlorine was closer, being only one flight upstairs, so he decided to start there.

17
Cl
Chlorine
35.45

He opened the door cautiously and immediately put his hand over his nose. "Whew! What a strong odor! Reminds me of my swimming pool in the summer," he thought.

The students in this room looked quite different than the metal atoms. The chlorine atoms were not shiny at all but were a dull green color, and they had fewer electrons than copper. They were dutifully reciting the lesson led by their teacher:

Chlorine is a useful gas,
And we're a pretty shade of green.
We hate germs and we hate dirt.
We disinfect and clean.

Chlorine has a pungent smell.
In fact, some say we stink.
But just a drop of chlorine makes
Your water safe to drink.

Chlorine atoms love to bond,
We're reactive to a fault.
Our favorite partner's sodium,
Together we make salt.

Like fluorine, bromine, iodine
Halogens are we.
We're greedy for electrons,
Grabbing every one we see.

Adam searched the room, looking for Ollie, but there was no sign of him. The chlorine atoms seemed oblivious to Adam's presence. They were too focused on the teacher. The smell of chlorine was very strong in the room, much stronger than Adam remembered from the swimming pool at the park. His eyes started to burn and fill with tears, which made it impossible for him to see clearly. How would he ever find Ollie?

Soon Adam's throat was burning and he couldn't stop coughing. The chlorine atoms, who hadn't noticed Adam at first, now turned around to stare. A few of them stood up to get a closer look at Adam, and they surrounded him near the back of the room. The smell was really strong now, and Adam felt dizzy. He was having trouble breathing, and he turned to look for the door. But his eyes were tearing so much that he couldn't see the door, and he kept getting dizzier, until the room was spinning so much he could feel himself starting to fall. Then everything went black.

From his hiding place under one of the desks, Ollie saw Adam fall. When Adam first entered the class, Ollie was the only one who saw him, since the chlorine atoms were all facing the other way. He had observed Adam with great curiosity, since Ollie had never seen an atom that looked anything like this creature—his head was much too small, and he had no electrons. Ollie wanted to get a closer look, but he also wanted to stay hidden; after his experience with the copper atoms at recess, Ollie wasn't keen on talking to any other elements for a while.

"Rust rat," he mumbled to himself. "Why did I have to be born an oxygen atom? Why couldn't I have been gold or silver or copper, or even aluminum or tin? Any metal would have been fine. But no, I have to be a reactive gas, and none of the popular atoms at school will play with me. It's not fair."

Ollie couldn't bear to return to his own class. As long as he stayed away, he couldn't finish his training, and he wouldn't be sent out to the world, locked forever as an oxygen atom. He wanted time to see if there was some way for him to change into something better than oxygen—preferably a metal. He often daydreamed about what it would be like to be a gold atom, and have all the other atoms in the Periodic School clamor to be his friend. The chlorine room was a good place to hide while he figured out his next step. And then he saw the newcomer fall to the floor.

Ollie's curiosity won out over his self-pity, and he climbed out from under the desk. One of the chlorine atoms turned to him in surprise, "Hey Ollie, what are you doing in here? Why aren't you up in your own room?"

Ollie recognized his cousin Clyde. Ollie didn't have to worry about being picked on by chlorine atoms. They were more reactive than he was, and most of the other atoms in the school tried to avoid them. If you got too close to a chlorine atom, you could find yourself bonded into a compound before you knew it.

"Oh, I just needed some time to myself, Clyde. Had a bit of a run-in with Connie at recess."

Ollie had no intention of explaining to Clyde his plan to avoid his own classroom and then find some way to change himself into a more popular element, preferably gold. Clyde nodded in sympathy; he had had his share of unpleasant encounters with Connie and her cronies himself.

"What's going on here?" asked Ollie.

"No idea," said Clyde. "This weird-looking atom wandered in here a few minutes ago, and when we came over to check him out, he just passed out. Want to take a look?"

Clyde nudged his friends away from Adam so Ollie could get a better look. Ollie had never seen an atom collapse before, and he knelt down to get a better view. Even though this creature was strange-looking, Ollie could sense that it shouldn't be lying so still.

"Step back," Ollie said to the chlorine atoms. "You know how irritating you guys can be—especially to elements that aren't used to working with you."

They seemed reluctant to move, too curious to see what would happen to the strange atom on the ground.

"Come on, guys, step back!" Ollie said sharply.

Clyde helped by gathering the crowd and ushering them to the front of the room, away from Adam. Ollie bent low over Adam and observed him closely. His face was very white, and his eyes were closed.

"Are you okay?" Ollie shouted into Adam's face.

After a few seconds, Adam's eyes flickered open, and he coughed. "Wh—what happened? Where am I?" He could barely get the words out because he was coughing so hard.

Come on," Ollie said. "We'd better get out of this room." As Ollie helped Adam stand up, he called to his cousin. "Thanks for the help, Clyde. I have a feeling that this element doesn't react well with chlorine."

Adam was still a little light-headed, so he was happy to let this new atom lead him out of the room. "I think you just saved my life," he whispered hoarsely. "I couldn't breathe in there."

Adam's head hurt, but he could tell that this atom did not look like the ones who had surrounded him just before he blacked out. "You're not a chlorine atom, are you? What element are you?"

Ollie hesitated. He didn't want to get teased again, and he had no idea whether this weird looking atom was part of the precious metal crowd.

Adam studied him carefully. He might not know as much chemistry as the atoms in the Periodic School, but he did know that oxygen is what people need to breathe. Wasn't that why Mrs. Gold sent him here in the first place? And didn't this atom help him breathe again?

"You're an oxygen atom, aren't you?" Adam asked. "You're Ollie! You're the one I've been looking for!"

Ollie backed away suspiciously. "Yeah, what of it? And who are *you*, anyway? I've never seen you around here before. What kind of atom are you? And where are your electrons?" Ollie took a step away from Adam.

"Wait, don't go. My name is Adam, and I am not an atom. I'm a boy. I've been sent here to find you."

"Find *me*? What are you talking about? What's a boy? How did you get here? Who sent you?" Ollie's questions tumbled out in a rush.

"My science teacher, Mrs. Gold, sent me."

Ollie's eyes opened wide at the word gold. "Gold? Did you say gold? Are you a gold atom? You sure don't look like a gold atom."

"No, Mrs. Gold isn't a gold atom, and neither am I. She is just a person, a human being, a teacher."

Ollie stared at Adam in confusion. Adam paused, uncertain how to explain what people were. He looked at his watch: there wasn't much time left. He had to convince Ollie to go back to his own classroom.

"Look, Ollie," Adam said gently. "I know what happened at recess …"

Ollie stiffened and backed away from Adam. "I don't want to talk about it," Ollie sputtered. He turned to walk away from Adam. He certainly didn't need the sympathy of a creature who didn't even have electrons.

"Wait, please!" Adam called out, desperate to keep Ollie talking. "My teacher, Mrs. Gold, isn't an atom, but she's an alchemist, and alchemists have magic powers. She's the one who shrunk me down to the size of an atom and sent me to the Periodic School to find you."

Ollie stopped at the word alchemist. "An alchemist? Really? We learned about alchemy in my class and how the alchemists tried to turn lead into gold, but my teacher says they don't exist any more."

"Mrs. Gold exists, and she is the real thing," Adam said. "I'm here, aren't I? You can tell that I come from a different world. She's the one who told me about you and ..." Adam hesitated. "... and the problem at recess."

Ollie flushed at the mention of recess, making his face purple. "I don't want to talk about recess. Tell me more about this Mrs. Gold. Is she really an alchemist? Does that mean she knows the art of transmutation? Could she change me into a precious metal?" asked Ollie eagerly. "You know, perform a real transmutation, just like we read about in school?"

Adam wasn't sure—Mrs. Gold hadn't said anything to him about changing elements, and he didn't know the word *transmutation*. "I don't think so," he told Ollie, "but anyway, you *can't* change. You need to get back to your own room."

"I still don't see why she is making such a big deal over one little oxygen atom," Ollie sniffed dismissively. "No one needs me. The metals can't even stand to be near me," whispered Ollie, remembering Connie's cruel taunt.

"Don't think about Connie, or those other metals," Adam counseled, the memory of Raymond flashing into his mind. "In my world, oxygen is one of the most important elements of all. Don't you realize what happened just now? You saved my life because people like me need oxygen to breathe. We can't live without you. And if you don't go back to your own classroom, pretty soon my world will run out of oxygen, and no one will be able to breathe, and then ..." Adam's voice dropped. "We'll all die, and you won't be able to save us."

"What are you talking about?" Ollie looked at Adam as if he was crazy. "What difference does it make if I go back to my classroom or not?"

"Don't you know the rules of your own school?" Adam couldn't hide his surprise. He wasn't used to knowing more than these atoms. "Mrs. Gold told me that the teachers here are not allowed to teach their classes unless all the students are present. So right now, your teacher and the other oxygen atoms in your class are waiting for you to come back. But there isn't much time, and if you don't go back, none of the oxygen atoms will graduate, and they won't be ready to go to my world to do their jobs. And no one will be able to breathe. Don't you see how important this is?" Adam was pleading now, and he reached out to put a hand on Ollie's arm.

Ollie recoiled from Adam's touch, but he hesitated. He knew that once he finished his lessons, he would be sent out to work forever as an oxygen atom, but he had never thought about where he would end up, or this rule about all the atoms having to be present.

"I'm not sure I believe you," Ollie finally said. "Why should I?"

Adam could sense the seconds ticking by, and he didn't seem to be making any headway with Ollie. Then he had an idea. He pulled the philosopher's stone from his pocket and showed it to Ollie.

"Because I have the philosopher's stone—that proves that Mrs. Gold is a real alchemist and my story is true."

Ollie stared at the little white stone. "Wow!" he said. "Is that really the philosopher's stone? That's what the alchemists were all looking for. According to my teacher, they thought it would turn other elements into gold."

Before Adam could respond, Ollie reached out, grabbed the stone, and sprinted to the stairs.

Adam was left standing alone in the hall, his empty hand held out in front of him.

CHAPTER EIGHT

It only took Adam a moment to recover from the shock of Ollie's action, and then he took off after him. As fast as Adam was, Ollie was still faster, and he disappeared before Adam could see where he was going. Frustrated, Adam stood in the stairway and listened closely for any clue as to where Ollie had gone. Then Adam heard a noise, and he was quite sure it came from upstairs. Running up the stairs, he thought how desperate his situation had become. Not only was the world in danger of running out of oxygen, but unless he got the stone back, he would be stuck in the Periodic School forever!

As Adam climbed the stairs, he realized there were still a lot of rooms where Ollie could be hiding, and he fought a sense of panic.

"I can't give up," he told himself. "Too many people are depending on me."

He took a deep breath, and pulled the periodic table out of his pocket. There were only two more rows in the Periodic School. Adam looked to see what was on Row 2. Immediately above chlorine, there was a square that said fluorine, and right next to it, a square for oxygen. That was Ollie's homeroom, and it was pretty clear that Ollie wouldn't be heading back there. Adam figured that Ollie would want to get as far away from his own room as he could, so he guessed that Ollie would climb to the top: Row 1. Luckily, there were only two rooms on the top floor: Helium and Hydrogen. He would have to check both.

When Adam emerged from the stairs onto Row 1, there was no sign of Ollie. Not that Adam was expecting to see him. He guessed that Ollie would be hiding in one of the rooms. He decided to start with helium.

```
2
He
Helium
4.003
```

Inside, the classroom looked much the same as the other rooms Adam had been in, but there was one big difference. The atoms were wearing seatbelts. Even the teacher was strapped to the desk. They were quite small, and Adam was finally able to see exactly how many electrons were circling their heads. Only two.

Adam scanned the room, searching for Ollie, but he did not see any sign of him. He bent down to look under the desks. Nothing. The atoms were so engrossed in their lessons that they didn't even notice Adam crouched on the floor.

They recited after their teacher:

> Have you ever lost balloons
> That floated to the sky?
> Or watched a giant blimp sail past
> And asked how it can fly?
>
> We're the answer: helium!
> Atomic mass of four.

We are lighter than the air
So your balloons can soar

Helium is mostly found
Inside the stars and sun.
In Greek, the sun's called Helios,
So we're called helium.

Other atoms envy us
For our stability.
We don't react, we don't form bonds.
A noble gas are we.

Adam was about to ask the teacher if he had seen Ollie when, all of a sudden, one of the girls in the back of the room loosened her seatbelt. As the teacher shouted, "Stop, Henrietta!" the girl floated up to the top of the room. She reminded Adam of the helium balloon that Mrs. Gold had talked about that afternoon.

The helium class burst out laughing, and the teacher had to bang his meter stick on the desk to restore order. It took quite a while to get Henrietta down into her seat, and Adam was practically shaking with impatience—there was so little time left, and this silly helium atom had wasted precious minutes. The teacher was quite upset about the interruption.

"What have I been teaching you all term?" he asked. "You are a noble gas. That means you are one of the most stable elements. You need to learn to act like a noble gas. And that means no fooling around!" The teacher sat down, exhausted.

Adam grabbed the moment to interrupt. "Please, sir," he said, using his most respectful tone, "have you seen an oxygen atom?"

The teacher looked up, remarkably unfazed by the sudden appearance of a boy in his class. He didn't even ask Adam where his electrons were.

"I'm looking for an atom of oxygen named Ollie," Adam explained. "Have you seen him? He ran away from his classroom, and I have to find him before my world runs out of oxygen."

"I wish I could help you," the teacher replied, "but no one has come into this room since early this morning when school began. Why don't you try asking the hydrogen teacher next door? He's been at the Periodic School longer than anyone and knows everything that happens here."

Adam thanked the teacher for his help and ran back out into the hall. He crossed his fingers and ran down to the room marked Hydrogen.

1

H

Hydrogen

1.008

CHAPTER NINE

The hydrogen atoms were even smaller than the helium atoms. They were also wearing seatbelts, and each atom had just one electron whizzing around its head.

"Well, that makes sense," Adam thought, remembering the chemistry lesson in his own school earlier in the day. "Hydrogen is also lighter than air."

Seemed like ages ago that he was sitting comfortably in his own chair at Rose Park Elementary School listening to Mrs. Gold explain the Periodic Table of elements. As he scanned the room, frantically looking for Ollie, he couldn't believe how upset he had been over a little soccer game, and the teasing of a dope like Raymond. With the fate of the world on his shoulders, missing a soccer goal seemed pretty trivial.

Adam looked under all the desks, but he didn't see Ollie. He *has* to be here, Adam thought. It is the only place that makes sense. He must be hiding somewhere.

The teacher looked up at Adam. "Can I help you?" he asked kindly. The teacher was a very old-looking atom, small and wrinkled, and he smiled warmly at Adam.

"I'm looking for an oxygen atom named Ollie," Adam explained breathlessly. "Have you seen him?"

"I didn't notice anyone entering," the teacher replied, "but then again, I've been busy writing the lesson on the board. Why don't you stick around for a few minutes? If an oxygen atom is hiding here, we'll know soon enough."

"But how?" asked Adam, looking helplessly about.

"Oh, you'll see," laughed the ancient little teacher.

The hydrogen atoms began their lesson:

> Although we are the smallest
> Atomic number one,
> It's the energy of hydrogen
> That fuels the stars and sun.
>
> Inside the sun it gets so hot
> We stick together tight.
> And then we fuse, in groups of twos,
> To make the sun shine bright.
>
> Unique among the elements
> We have no family.
> We like our one electron,
> But lose it frequently.
>
> We join with oxygen to form
> The compound H_2O.
> And when the bonding is complete,
> Just watch the water flow.

Just as the class was finishing the lesson, one of the hydrogen atoms squealed happily and loosened her seatbelt. Adam watched in amazement as she floated to the top of the classroom. Then Adam saw why: Ollie was crouched on top of a high shelf of books, and the hydrogen atom was heading right toward him.

Soon other hydrogen atoms were floating up to join her. Two of them grabbed onto Ollie, and Ollie started yelling: "Let go! Let go!"

At first Adam didn't understand why Ollie sounded so frightened, but then he saw something strange. Right before his eyes, it looked like Ollie was melting into a puddle of water.

"Let go of him!" ordered the teacher.

The hydrogen atoms reluctantly released Ollie, and they floated gently back to their seats.

"I told you we would find Ollie if he were hiding in this room. These hydrogens just can't resist trying to bond with oxygen atoms," the teacher explained. "They find them incredibly attractive."

"Come on down, Ollie," the teacher said gently. "I think you'd better go with this nice young ..." The teacher hesitated. "What did you say you were?" he asked Adam.

"A boy," Adam mumbled and walked out into the hall to wait for Ollie before the teacher could ask him any more questions.

Ollie reluctantly climbed down and walked out the door. He could hear the hydrogens giggling as he left. "Silly atoms," he grumbled to Adam. "I think that being lighter than air makes them act like air heads."

"Speaking of air heads, why did you take the philosopher's stone from me? Don't you know I can't get home without it? Come on. Give it back. It's no use to you. It won't turn you into gold."

Adam fought to keep his voice steady, but his frustration was starting to show. Ollie just stood there staring at his feet. Adam was stumped. He didn't know how to convince Ollie to give him the stone, much less go back to his own room. Time was running out, and Adam didn't seem any closer to solving this problem than he had been when he first found himself on the grass outside the Periodic School.

"Listen, Ollie," Adam began, when he was suddenly startled by a loud fire alarm. Ollie looked up, his eyes wide and bright. Almost immediately Adam saw the helium teacher calmly leading his class to the stairwell.

"What's going on?" Adam yelled.

The helium teacher paused at the door to the stairwell, gently prodding his little pupils down the stairs. "The phosphorus atoms on Row 3 were practicing their role in matches, and one them got too enthusiastic and caught fire. We have to leave the building immediately. Fires are very dangerous at the Periodic School. If we're not careful, other elements may ignite."

Adam turned to Ollie, who seemed frozen to the spot. "Come on. There is no time to argue now. We've got to get outside."

Adam had been through enough fire drills at Rose Park Elementary School to know how important it was to find an exit. But Ollie just stood there, refusing to answer or move. Adam couldn't tell if Ollie was paralyzed with fear of the fire or whether he was still angry with Adam for following him to the hydrogen classroom.

"Ollie, please, didn't you hear what the helium teacher just said? We have to go!"

Ollie remained as still as a statue. Adam looked around; he did not smell any smoke yet, but he did not doubt the danger that he was in. He was torn between the desire to race to the nearest stairway and get outside where he would be safe and the need to stay close to Ollie.

The helium atoms were almost all gone now, and Adam watched the teacher take the hand of the last student and walk him down the stairs. Adam noticed that the door to the hydrogen room was closed. Why weren't the hydrogen atoms trying to escape like the helium atoms? Adam wondered. He carefully opened the door.

Inside, all the hydrogen atoms were huddled against the wall farthest from the door. They looked terrified.

"Close the door! Close the door!" the teacher shouted in alarm. "Don't you realize what will happen if the fire reaches these atoms? We'll explode!"

Some of the little hydrogen atoms were crying. Adam stared at them for a moment, and then he looked back at Ollie, who was just visible outside the door. Suddenly, Adam had an idea.

"Come in here, Ollie, quick!" Adam shouted.

Ollie was so surprised that he followed Adam's order without a protest.

"Remember what happened when the hydrogen atoms latched on to you?" he asked Ollie breathlessly. You made *water!*"

The hydrogen teacher jumped up and ran over to Adam. "Of course," he said. "How could I have been so stupid? How could I have forgotten about making H_2O? If we get more oxygen atoms up here, we can make enough water to put out the fire. Adam, you're brilliant. Wait here while I go and get the other oxygen atoms."

"No," said Adam hastily, "That's too dangerous for you. You stay here with the little ones, and I will find the other oxygen atoms."

And before Ollie or the teacher had time to protest, Adam was out the door, the periodic table in his hand, racing for the stairs to Row 2. There was nothing that they could do now but wait and hope.

Within seconds, Adam was back in the hydrogen room, followed by a bunch of atoms who looked exactly like Ollie. They greeted Ollie happily, exchanging hugs and high fives.

"No time for that," Adam urged, "You've got work to do."

The two teachers organized the atoms of hydrogen and oxygen into little groups of three: two hydrogens with each oxygen. As they hurried out the door, Adam could see them turning into water. As the room emptied, Adam took a second to check under the desks and on top of the shelves to make sure there were no stragglers and then quickly took off after them. No need for the map—the wet trail would lead him right to the fire.

Adam followed the oxygen-hydrogen groups downstairs. The smoke seemed much thinner in their wake, so he could see what was happening. On the third row, all the other atoms were rushing down the stairs to get away from the fire, but the determined oxygen-hydrogens headed right toward Room 15, where the fire had started.

Adam hurried after them. He watched in relief as water poured into Room 15 and sprayed out into the hall, soaking him through and through. The building was saved! The fire was out!

Adam collapsed from exhaustion and relief and sat down right there in the hallway. He didn't mind the water dripping down his forehead into his eyes as he listened to the yelps of glee all around him. He closed his eyes and smiled.

CHAPTER TEN

Adam leaned against the wall, too exhausted to move. The fire was out, and the atoms were slowly drifting back to their classes. He could hear them chattering about the fire, how dumb the phosphorus atom had been, and how thrilling it was to hear the gush of water just in time.

Adam wasn't the only one who had been really scared when the alarm sounded. But he felt a huge surge of pride in his quick thinking. He hadn't panicked. He knew what to do! Maybe he didn't know as much about the elements and chemistry as the atoms did, but he was the one who figured out how to put out the fire. Just wait till Sam heard about this!

And then Adam remembered that Sam was far away, and he still had not convinced Ollie to return to his own classroom. Sure, Ollie had helped put out the fire, but what if he disappeared again? What if he was still upset about being an oxygen atom and kept the philosopher's stone thinking it would change him to gold? Things looked pretty bleak. Not only had he failed Mrs. Gold, but also he had no idea how he was going to get home.

Just then, he heard someone laughing. He looked up in surprise, and there was Ollie, standing right in front of him.

"Looking for this?" Ollie chuckled, holding out his hand.

To Adam's great relief, there lay the philosopher's stone, safe and sound. Adam carefully took the philosopher's stone and put it securely back in his pocket.

"Wh—wh—what are you doing here?" Adam stuttered in astonishment.

Ollie laughed again. "Looks like you won the argument after all. I've decided to go back to my own classroom."

Adam looked quizzically at Ollie.

"Well, it seems that you were right about how important I am," Ollie said. "Oxygen is the hero of the day around here, and all the elements are congratulating us for saving the school. Maybe being an oxygen isn't such a bad thing, after all. And anyway, I finally figured out that you were right about this philosopher's stone. It won't turn me into gold."

Adam jumped up, and without thinking, gave Ollie a huge hug.

"Whoa, there, Adam not Atom, let's not get carried away."

"Sorry," Adam said. "I'm just so glad to hear that you are going back to your class. What happened to the water?"

"Oh, once the fire was out, we separated from the hydrogens, and everyone is back in their own classrooms again."

Adam looked puzzled.

"Atoms don't bond forever, you know," Ollie explained. "Compounds can separate back into the original elements."

"How?"

"Never mind," Ollie said, laughing. "You better go back to your own school and learn more about chemistry."

It took Adam a minute to absorb the significance of what Ollie was telling him. He had succeeded in his mission for Mrs. Gold! Everything was back to normal in the Periodic School, and there was no longer any danger that his world would run out of oxygen to breathe! He felt relieved and happy and exhausted, all at the same time. He just stood there smiling at Ollie, who beamed with pride.

"Come on," Ollie said. "Before you leave, why don't you walk me back to my classroom and check out some really important atoms!"

Adam was anxious to get home, but he didn't want to hurt Ollie's feelings, so he followed him to the oxygen classroom. The sign on the door read:

$$\boxed{\begin{array}{c} 8 \\ O \\ \text{Oxygen} \\ 16.00 \end{array}}$$

Adam paused at the door. "Before we go in, could I ask you a favor?"

"Depends what it is," replied Ollie cautiously.

Adam pointed to the door. "Well, I've been looking at these signs on the doors of your school all day, and I can't figure out what the numbers and symbols mean. I recognize the names of the elements, but what is the other stuff?"

"That's easy," said Ollie. "The first number is the atomic number—that tells how many protons and electrons we have. See, I have eight electrons," explained Ollie, pointing to his head. "Underneath is the symbol we use for an element—kind of like a code. And the bottom number is our atomic weight. That includes protons and neutrons. Get it?"

"Sort of," Adam said slowly. "I still have lots of questions, but I'll save them for Mrs. Gold."

Inside the classroom, Adam saw the familiar array of desks. At each one sat an atom that looked exactly like Ollie.

"How can we ever thank you, Adam?" the teacher gushed. Turning to Ollie, he spoke sternly, "I hope you've learned your lesson, Ollie. You can't pay attention to the teasing of those metals. Yes, they are beautiful, but so are you, in your own way. And being able to bond is an important trait. Just think what would have happened if we hadn't been able to bond so well with hydrogen."

"Well, I still think it would be cool to be an element like gold," said Ollie.

The teacher frowned.

Ollie took a seat right in front of the room. "But for now," Ollie told him, "oxygen is the element to be."

"As for you, Adam" the teacher continued, "I have an idea for a little thank you gift. We've all been feeling a little sorry for you because you don't have any electrons."

Adam instinctively put his hand up to his head.

"So we've gathered up some loose electrons for you and put them in this vial. Now you have your very own. When you figure out your atomic number, you can count out the right number for your head."

Adam didn't bother explaining to the teacher that he had no atomic number. "Thank you very much," he said solemnly.

"All right, class," the teacher spoke crisply to the students. "We've lost a lot of time today."

Ollie flushed with embarrassment as his teacher looked pointedly at him.

"We better get moving with our lesson."

As he led the class, Adam could hear Ollie's voice above all the others:

> Oxygen is in the air,
> But it's hard to tell.
> We have no color, have no taste,
> And we have no smell.
>
> People need us just to breathe,
> And there is no doubt.
> Oxygen is an element
> You cannot live without.
>
> Oxygen makes fires burn.
> And we make metals rust.

With silicon we form the rocks
That cover the earth's crust.

We join with hydrogen to form
The compound H_2O.
And when the bonding is complete,
Just watch the water flow.

As the lesson ended, Adam reached into his pocket and pulled out the philosopher's stone. Time to go home! He held it tightly in his hand, and then he froze. Oh no! He had completely forgotten the verse that Mrs. Gold had taught him to recite! So much had happened since he arrived at the Periodic School that the words had disappeared from his brain!

CHAPTER ELEVEN

Adam stood perfectly still, fighting the panic that was growing in his chest. He knew he had to stay calm or he would never have a chance of remembering.

Ollie turned around to wave goodbye to Adam and was surprised to see Adam standing rigid and pale in the back of the room. He ran over to see what was wrong.

"I can't remember the verse my teacher taught me to get back home," Adam told Ollie in a strangled voice. "I know I have to recite the names of three elements and then say, 'Mendeleev, take me home,' but I can't remember the elements."

"Calm down," Ollie said. "You found me, didn't you? I'm sure we can figure this out. Did your teacher give you any hints?"

Adam closed his eyes and pictured Mrs. Gold in his familiar classroom back at Rose Park Elementary School. A memory came back to him. Mrs. Gold had said something about the noble gases.

"She told me to think of the noble gases," he said.

"Aha," said Ollie. "That's a good hint. There aren't too many noble gases. Good thing she didn't tell you to think of a metal!"

"This is no time to joke around," Adam told Ollie frantically.

"Okay, okay, just stay calm. Now there are six noble gases: Radon, xenon, krypton, argon, neon, and helium. Do any of those sound familiar?"

"Helium sounds familiar," replied Adam. "But that may be because I just visited their room."

"Think harder," encouraged Ollie.

Adam screwed up his face as he concentrated on remembering Mrs. Gold's instructions. "I am pretty sure she didn't mention krypton. I would have remembered that, because it sounds like kryptonite. You know, the stuff that kills Superman?"

"Superman?" Ollie repeated quizzically.

"Never mind," Adam said. "And xenon is also such a weird name, I think I would have recognized it."

"Okay," Ollie said with satisfaction. "Now we're getting somewhere. Let's try a few combinations."

Adam held the philosopher's stone firmly and said:

"Radon, argon, neon,
Mendeleev, take me home."

Nothing happened.

"That didn't sound right," said Ollie. "Try again."

Adam dutifully recited a different combination.

"Helium, neon, argon,
Mendeleev, take me home."

Still nothing.

"Try helium at the end," suggested Ollie. "I think that has a nice ring to it."

Adam tried closing his eyes.

"Neon, argon, helium,
Mendeleev, take me home."

Again nothing happened.

"I have an idea," said Ollie. "Reverse argon and neon. That way, you'll be saying them in order of largest to smallest."

Adam sighed. He was willing to try anything. Once again Adam clutched the philosopher's stone tightly in his hand and recited:

> "Argon, neon, helium,
>
> Mendeleev, take me home."

Suddenly Adam felt the walls spinning around him, and he barely had time to yell, "Thanks Ollie!" before he was lifted off the ground once again. This time the swirling cloud of bright light filled him with relief, not fear. He smiled as the walls of the Periodic School faded away and he spun around, knowing he was on his way home.

He opened his eyes to see Mrs. Gold looking down at him as he sat at his desk.

"Wake up Adam," she said, "I'm ready to talk to you now about being late."

Adam rubbed his eyes. "But Mrs. Gold, don't you want to hear what happened to Ollie?"

"Ollie?"

"It wasn't easy," Adam said. "It took a long time to find him, and the gold atoms were really stuck up, and the silver atom wasn't much better, but I think the copper atom, Connie, was the worst of all. She was so mean to Ollie. I could understand why he ran away. But then the fire broke out, and I had to get the oxygen atoms together with …"

"Hold on, Adam, you are not making any sense."

Adam stood up. "Don't worry, Mrs. Gold. I won't tell anyone that you're an alchemist."

"Why, of course I'm no alchemist, Adam. There haven't been any alchemists for hundreds of years. Whatever made you think of that?"

Adam stared at her and then glanced at his desk, where his papers were in disarray, and some books had fallen on the floor. "But it was real," he whispered to himself, "I know it was real."

"What's that, dear?" Mrs. Gold helped him pick up his books. "You have to speak up. My hearing isn't what it used to be."

"Nothing," Adam mumbled, too confused to argue. "So, what's my punishment?"

"It took me a while to think of something appropriate," she responded, "but I have the perfect assignment. I want you to write a paper about the element oxygen and why it is so important for life on earth."

Adam's head snapped up and he studied Mrs. Gold's face intently. "Why oxygen?" he asked.

"Oh, I don't know. It just seemed like the perfect element for you to write about." Her face was serious, but Adam could swear her eyes were twinkling with amusement. "You can give the essay to me tomorrow, Adam. Have a good afternoon."

And she walked back to her desk.

Adam gathered his books together and stuffed them into his backpack, too confused to say anything. The dream had been so real, and he could remember every detail. That never happened when he dreamt at night. He put his head down and jammed his hands into his pockets as he walked toward the door.

But he stopped suddenly as he felt a smooth, round object. Pulling it out, he recognized the philosopher's stone that Mrs. Gold had given him. Just underneath it was a tiny vial filled with glowing light.

"Electrons," he whispered to himself. He turned to see Mrs. Gold, who had stopped grading papers and was watching him closely.

Adam held up the stone. "I think this is yours, Mrs. Gold."

Without saying a word, Mrs. Gold opened her desk drawer, pulled out a small canvas bag and held it open with both hands. Adam slowly walked up to her and looked her right in the eyes. He hesitated, holding the stone tightly in his hand, reluctant to let it go. Finally he sighed and dropped the stone into the sack. She gave him the tiniest smile as she pulled the drawstring closed and replaced the sack in her desk.

"I'll see you tomorrow, Adam. We'll be learning about protons, neutrons, and electrons. Should be a piece of cake for a budding chemist like you."

Adam smiled back, touching the vial of electrons in his pocket. "You bet, Mrs. Gold."

The Periodic Table of the Elements

1 **H** 1.01								
3 **Li** 6.94	4 **Be** 9.01							
11 **Na** 22.99	12 **Mg** 24.31							
19 **K** 39.10	20 **Ca** 40.08	21 **Sc** 44.96	22 **Ti** 47.87	23 **V** 50.94	24 **Cr** 51.99	25 **Mn** 54.94	26 **Fe** 55.85	27 **Co** 58.93
37 **Rb** 85.47	38 **Sr** 87.62	39 **Y** 88.91	40 **Zr** 91.22	41 **Nb** 92.91	42 **Mo** 95.94	43 **Tc** 98	44 **Ru** 101.1	45 **Rh** 102.9
55 **Cs** 132.9	56 **Ba** 137.3	57 **La** 138.9	72 **Hf** 178.5	73 **Ta** 180.9	74 **W** 183.8	75 **Re** 186.2	76 **Os** 190.2	77 **Ir** 192.2
87 **Fr** **223**	88 **Ra** 226	89 **Ac** 227	104 **Rf** 261	105 **Db** 262	106 **Sg** 263	107 **Bh** 262	108 **Hs** 265	109 **Mt** 266

58 **Ce** 140.1	59 **Pr** 140.9	60 **Nd** 144.2	61 **Pm** 145	62 **Sm** 150.4
90 **Th** 232.0	91 **Pa** 231.0	92 **U** 238.0	93 **Np** 237	94 **Pu** 244

								2 He 4.003
			5 B 10.81	6 C 12.01	7 N 14.01	8 O 15.99	9 F 18.99	10 Ne 20.18
			13 Al 26.98	14 Si 28.08	15 P 30.97	16 S 32.07	17 Cl 35.45	18 Ar 39.95
28 Ni 58.69	29 Cu 63.55	30 Zn 65.39	31 Ga 69.72	32 Ge 72.61	33 As 74.92	34 Se 78.96	35 Br 79.90	36 Kr 83.80
46 Pd 106.4	47 Ag 107.9	48 Cd 112.4	49 In 114.8	50 Sn 118.7	51 Sb 121.8	52 Te 127.6	53 I 126.9	54 Xe 131.3
78 Pt 195.1	79 Au 196.9	80 Hg 200.6	81 Tl 204.4	82 Pb 207.2	83 Bi 208.9	84 Po 209	85 At 210	86 Rn 222
110 Uun	111 Uuu	112 Uub						

63 Eu 151.9	64 Gd 157.2	65 Tb 158.9	66 Dy 162.5	67 Ho 164.9	68 Er 167.3	69 Tm 168.9	70 Yb 173.0	71 Lu 174.9
95 Am 243	96 Cm 247	97 Bk 247	98 Cf 251	99 Es 252	100 Fm 257	101 Md 258	102 No 259	103 Lr 262

978-0-595-45616-1
0-595-45616-2

Made in the USA
Middletown, DE
24 July 2017